Playing from the Heart

to Sarah
and Henry

ISBN 978-1-338-18845-5

12 11 10 9 8 7 6 5   19 20 21 22

Printed in the U.S.A.   169

First Scholastic printing, March 2017

This book was hand-lettered by Peter H. Reynolds.

The illustrations were done in pen, ink, watercolor, gouache, and tea.

Playing from the Heart

PETER H. REYNOLDS

SCHOLASTIC INC.

The piano stood quietly
in the living room for years.

Until the day Raj first plunked and pushed the keys, delighted by every sound.

As he got older, his legs could reach the
sustain pedal and the notes flowed.
Raj noticed that he could mix the notes
the way he mixed his watercolors.

His father heard the dreamy music
floating through the house. He was amazed
that his son was playing beautifully without
ever having taken a lesson.

His father was so impressed that he hired
a piano teacher to nurture Raj's talent.

They began the lesson.

Raj's teacher showed him that the sounds
he had been making had a way of being written.
They hung on bars stretching across the page.
These notes reminded him of zoo animals
peering through bars...wanting to escape.

Raj was a good student. He worked hard. His father was pleased when he heard songs he could recognize.

As the years passed, the songs became more familiar. Crisp and precise.

Although Raj played better and better

he got more and more tired...

until the day that even looking
at the piano made him exhausted.

Finally, Raj closed the cover over the keys. He was finished. The piano was silent.

Years passed, and Raj grew up and went to work in the city.

Raj's father was surprised how quiet the house was without his son.

Raj worked hard. He was diligent and focused. Then one night he got a call letting him know that his father was not well.

"Tell my father: I'm coming home."

Raj asked if there was anything he could do to comfort him.

"Could you play a song for me?"

Raj began playing
a piece he still remembered.

"No...not that one..." his father called out.
"The song without a name."

Raj found the sustain pedal and dove into a place he had not been in many years. The notes emerged whispery and sweet.

"Yes, yes...that's the one."
Raj's father closed his eyes and
savored the lingering notes.

Raj kept playing... from the heart.